Good night

Catherine and Laurence Anholt

little ORCHARD

Playing games since early morning.

250936

This book is to be returned on or before
the last date stamped below. Pi-3

LIBREX

F
ADA

Falkirk Council

For Brodie

ORCHARD BOOKS
96 Leonard Street, London EC2A 4XD
Orchard Books Australia
14 Mars Road, Lane Cove, NSW 2066
1 83069 187 7 (hardback)
1 84121 303 9 (paperback)
First published in Great Britain in 1999
Copyright text © Laurence Anholt 1999
Copyright illustrations © Catherine Anholt 1999
The rights of Laurence Anholt to be identified as the author and Catherine Anholt
as the illustrator of this work have been asserted by them in accordance
with the Copyright, Designs and Patents Act, 1988.
A CIP catalogue record for this book is available from the British Library.
Printed in Italy

Now we're tired, baby's yawning.

Muddy clothes all in a heap.

Bubbly water, warm and deep.

Rub-a-dub and wriggle jiggle.

Tickly tummy, giggle giggle.

Brush your teeth to keep them white.

Help me get my buttons right.

Much too tired to walk myself.

Choose a story from the shelf.

Jumping, bouncing in the air.

A picture book for us to share.

Give a kiss and say 'Good night'.

One last cuddle, squeeze me tight.

Close your eyes. No more peeping.

Quiet now, it's time for sleeping.